The Very Worst Monster

PAT HUTCHINS

The Very Worst Monster

MULBERRY BOOKS

New York

Printed in the United States of America
10 9 8 7 6 5 4 3 2
First Mulberry Edition, 1988

Library of Congress Cataloging in Publication Data

Hutchins, Pat, (date)
The very worst monster.
Summary: Hazel sets out to prove
that she, not her baby brother,
is the worst monster anywhere.
(1. Monsters—Fiction.
2. Brothers and sisters—
Fiction) I. Title.
PZ7.H96165Ve 1985   (E)   84-5928
ISBN 0-688-07816-8

FOR AMY

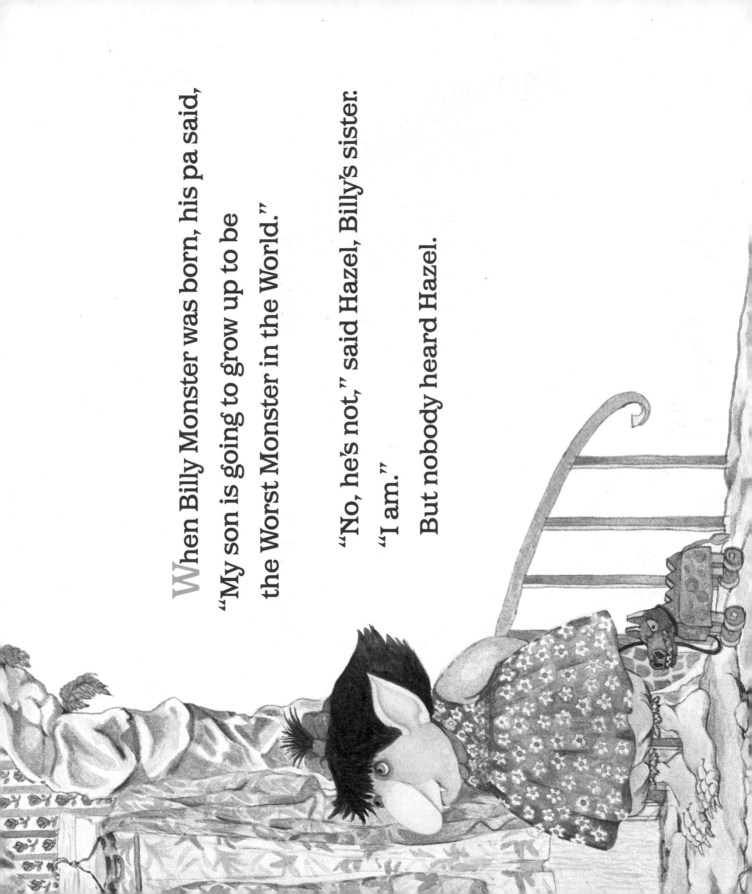

When Billy Monster was born, his pa said,

"My son is going to grow up to be the Worst Monster in the World."

"No, he's not," said Hazel, Billy's sister.

"I am."

But nobody heard Hazel.

When Grandpa and Grandma Monster
came to visit the baby, Grandpa said,

"Look at those strong fangs!

He can bend bars with his teeth!"

"So can I," said Hazel.

But they were all so busy

watching Billy that

nobody watched Hazel.

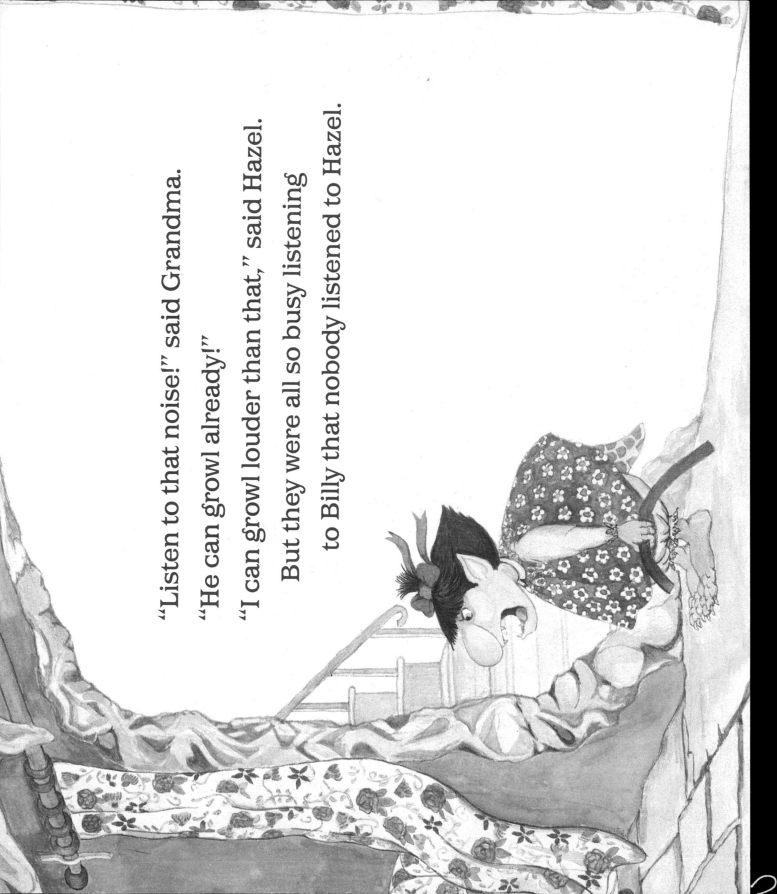

"Listen to that noise!" said Grandma.

"He can growl already!"

"I can growl louder than that," said Hazel.

But they were all so busy listening

to Billy that nobody listened to Hazel.

"Look," said Pa. "See how he swings
on the curtains!"

"I can do that," said Hazel.

But they were all so busy looking at Billy
that nobody looked at Hazel.

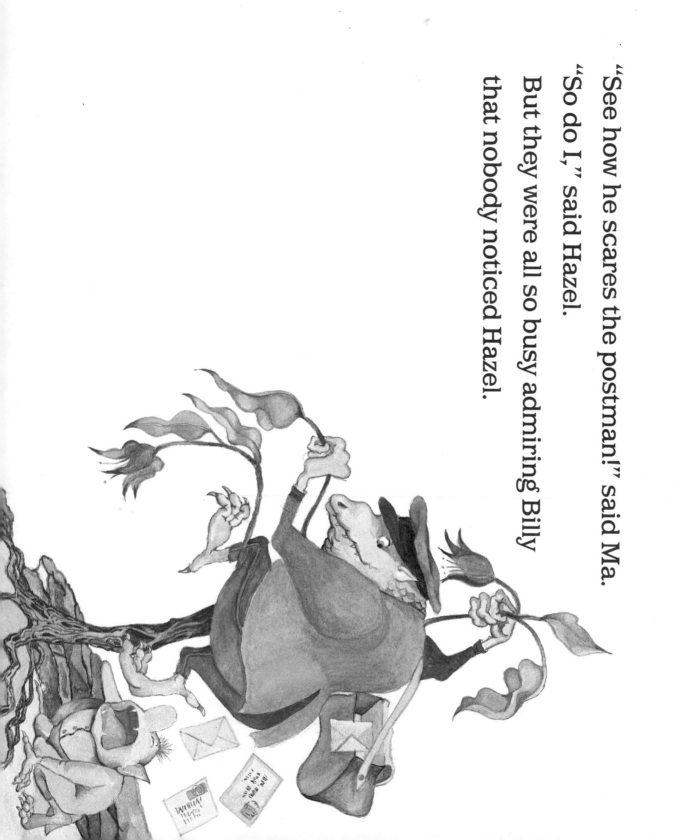

"See how he scares the postman!" said Ma.

"So do I," said Hazel.

But they were all so busy admiring Billy
that nobody noticed Hazel.

Ma and Pa thought Billy was such a bad baby
that they entered him in the
"Worst Monster Baby in the World" competition.

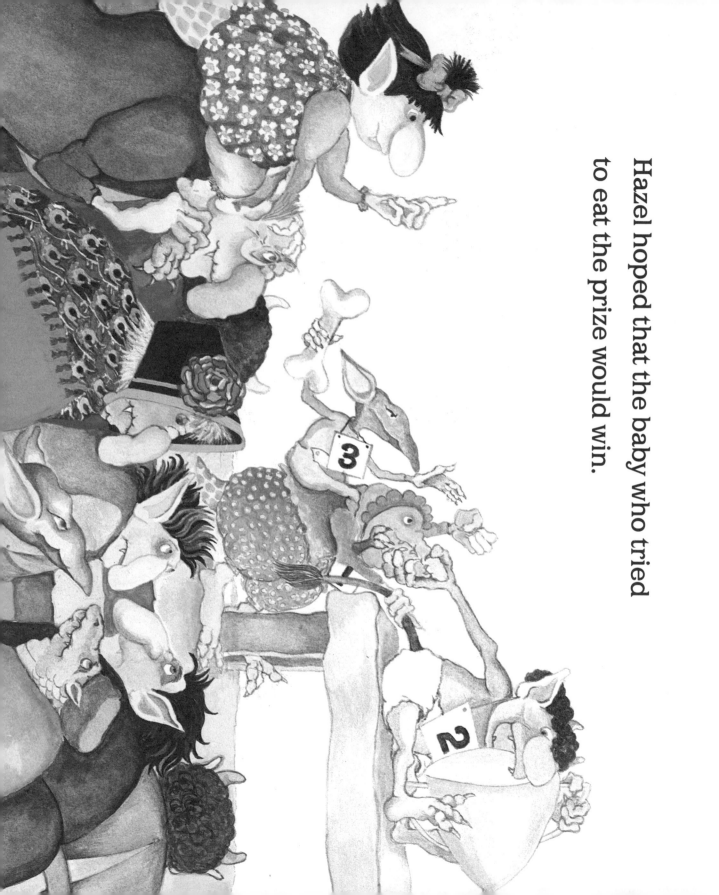

Hazel hoped that the baby who tried to eat the prize would win.

But then Billy tried to eat the judge.

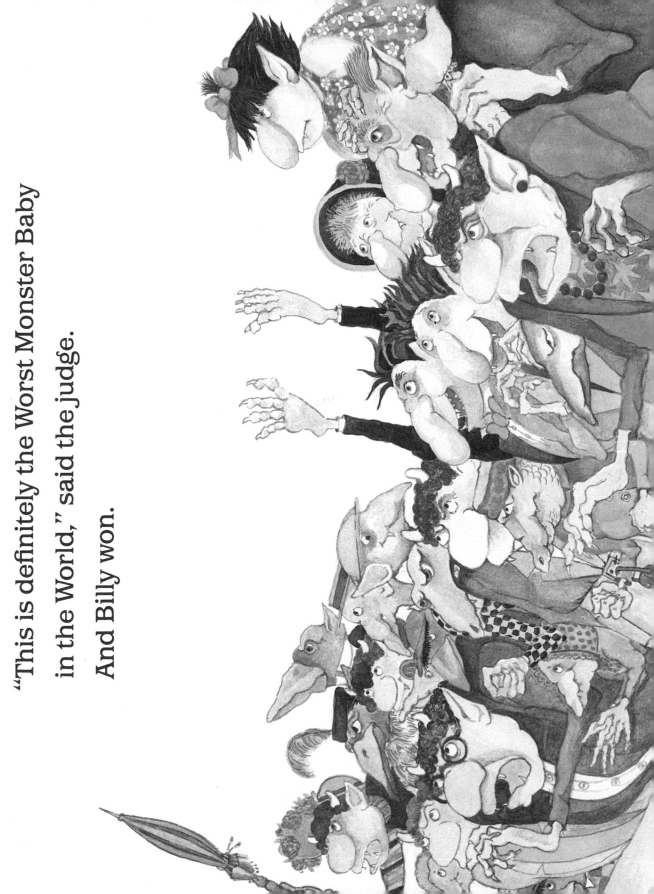

"This is definitely the Worst Monster Baby

in the World," said the judge.

And Billy won.

Ma and Pa and Grandma and Grandpa
were very proud of Billy.

"I know that he will grow up to be the
Worst Monster in the World,"
said Pa happily.

"No, he won't," said Hazel.
But nobody heard Hazel.

Hazel tried losing her little brother,

but he kept turning up again.

She tried frightening him away,
but that didn't work either.

So she gave him away.

"Where's Billy?" asked Ma and Pa.

"I gave him away," said Hazel.

"Oh!" cried Ma and Pa.

"You gave your own baby brother away!

You must be the Worst Monster

in the World!"

"I told you I was," said Hazel.

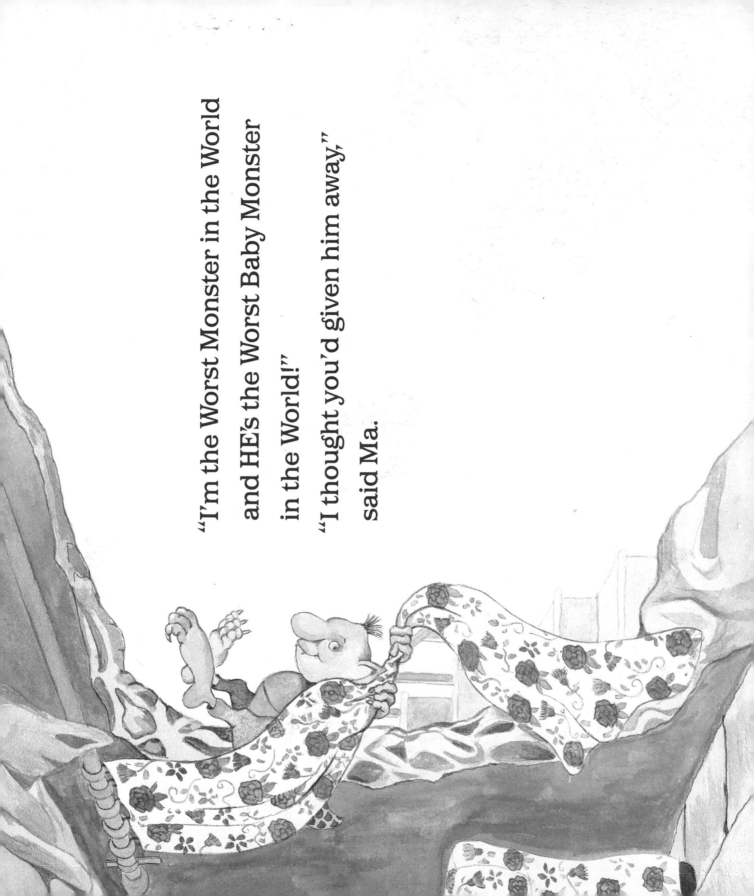

"I'm the Worst Monster in the World
and HE's the Worst Baby Monster
in the World!"

"I thought you'd given him away,"
said Ma.

"I did," said Hazel.
"But they gave him back!"